Sounds Like Christmas

Sounds Like Christmas

Robert Munsch

Illustrated by
Michael Martchenko

North Winds Press
An Imprint of Scholastic Canada Ltd.

The art for this book was painted in watercolour on Crescent illustration board.
The type is set in ITC Galliard.

Library and Archives Canada Cataloguing in Publication

Title: Sounds like Christmas / Robert Munsch ; illustrated by Michael Martchenko.

Names: Munsch, Robert N., 1945- author. | Martchenko, Michael, illustrator.

Identifiers: Canadiana 20190158441 | ISBN 9781443175821 (hardcover)

Classification: LCC PS8576.U575 S68 2019 | DDC jC813/.54—dc23

www.scholastic.ca

ISBN 978-1-4431-7582-1

7 6 5 4 3 2   Printed in Canada 114   20 21 22 23 24

FSC
www.fsc.org

MIX
Paper from
responsible sources
FSC® C016245

For Georgia Grace Grebenc, Niagara-on-the-Lake, Ontario;
Lincoln Joseph Grebenc, Ottawa, Ontario;
and Sharon Bruder, Guelph, Ontario.
— R.M.

Because Grandma was busy baking Christmas cookies, she said, "Georgia and Lincoln, will you please decorate the tree."

So Lincoln put on the lights and Georgia put on the garlands.

Then Georgia put on the candy canes and Lincoln put on the coloured balls.

It was a wonderful tree.

When all the regular stuff was up on the tree, Georgia said, "Watch this, I have something really neat."

She went upstairs and brought down a little blue bird that looked almost real.

"I saved up my allowance for this," said Georgia. She put it on the tree and pressed one leg and the blue bird started singing:

TWEET! TWEET! TWEET!

"Well, I have something better than that," said Lincoln. He went upstairs and brought down his sound effects key chain and hung it on the tree. It went:
BZAP! BZAP! BZAP!

"No fair," said Georgia. "That was not a real ornament!"

"It is now," said Lincoln.

So Georgia went upstairs and brought down a talking doll. She turned it on and stuck it on the tree. The doll said:

MA-MA! MA-MA! MA-MA!

"Beat that!" said Georgia.

Lincoln heard the neighbour's dog barking out in the street. The dog was an excellent barker, so Lincoln grabbed it and hung it on the Christmas tree. This worked really well, because the dog barked even louder than usual.

WOOF! WOOF! WOOF!

"Beat that!" said Lincoln.

Then their grandmother came in, looked at the tree, and yelled, *"AAHHHHHHHHHHHH!"*

It was a most wonderful and loud yell, so Georgia and Lincoln grabbed her and stuck her on the tree.

Now the tree was making a really incredible, tremendous racket, going:

TWEET! TWEET! TWEET!
BZAP! BZAP! BZAP!
MA-MA! MA-MA! MA-MA!
WOOF! WOOF! WOOF!
AAHHHHHHHHHHHH!

Finally their grandfather heard the racket. He had been out clearing the driveway and he ran inside with the snow blower still running.

GRRRRRRRRRRRRRR!
He was yelling, "STOP! STOP! STOP!"

19

He was making such a wonderful noise that Lincoln and Georgia grabbed him and stuck him at the very top of the tree, where the angel is supposed to go.

So the tree stood there making an incredible racket while Lincoln and Georgia marvelled at the sound they had created.

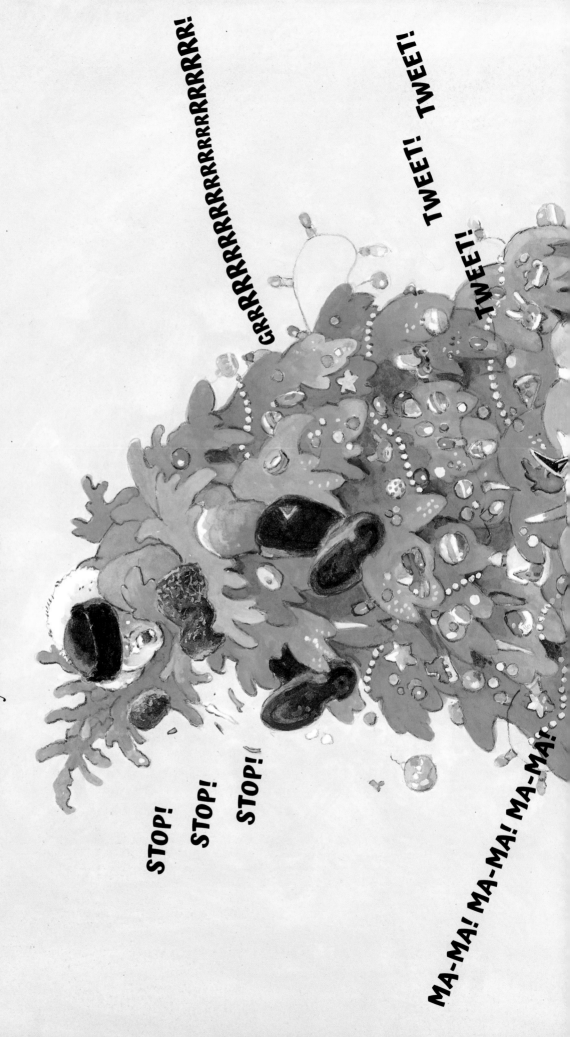

But finally the bird ran down and the key chain ran down and the doll ran down and the dog went to sleep and Grandma got hoarse and the snow blower ran out of gas, and their grandfather decided to try talking.

He said, "Now you know, if you don't get us down from this tree there will be nobody to give you presents."

"Ha!" said Lincoln. "I guess he never heard of Santa Claus." And Lincoln and Georgia went to finish baking the Christmas cookies.